The Christmas Light

Claudia Cangilla McAdam
ILLUSTRATED BY IGOR KOVYAR

SOPHIA INSTITUTE PRESS
Manchester, NH

A free discussion and activities
guide for this book is available at
www.ClaudiaMcAdam.com

SOPHIA
INSTITUTE PRESS

Printed in the United States of America.

Sophia Institute Press®
Box 5284, Manchester, NH 03108
1-800-888-9344

www.SophiaInstitute.com
Sophia Institute Press® is a registered trademark of Sophia Institute.

ISBN: 978-1-64413-113-8

Library of Congress Control Number: 2021940115

First printing, 2021

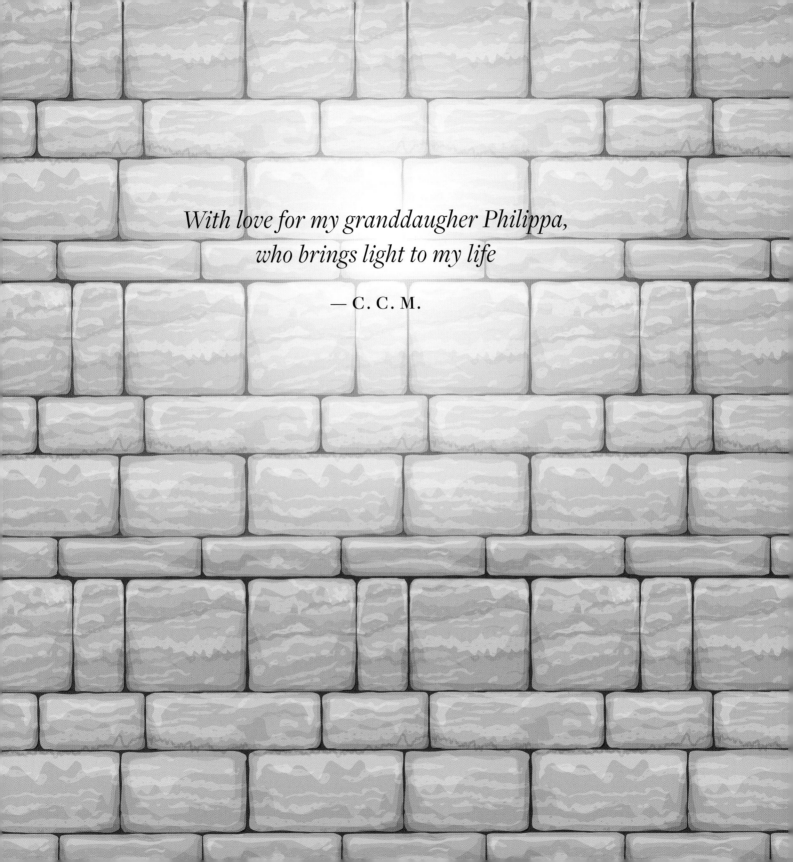

With love for my granddaugher Philippa,
who brings light to my life

— C. C. M.

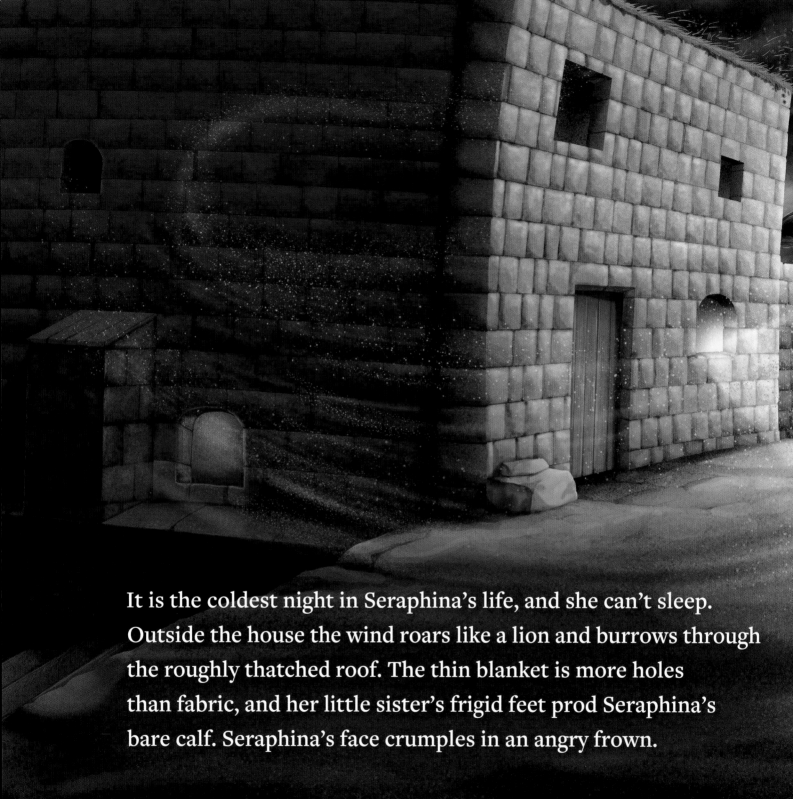

It is the coldest night in Seraphina's life, and she can't sleep. Outside the house the wind roars like a lion and burrows through the roughly thatched roof. The thin blanket is more holes than fabric, and her little sister's frigid feet prod Seraphina's bare calf. Seraphina's face crumples in an angry frown.

On a normal night, the children would not be so far from the fire, crowded in the loft, side by side like stones in a wall. But this is not a normal night.

Seraphina shoves her sister's feet away and stomps
down the ladder. Their tiny house is crammed
with family and strangers from out of town.

She tiptoes around the slumbering grown-ups, packed as tightly together on the floor as salted fish in a crate.

Seraphina opens the door a crack. The
icy hand of winter strikes her face.
Across the lane is their stable, a cave.

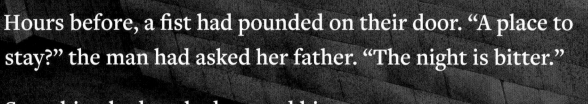

Hours before, a fist had pounded on their door. "A place to stay?" the man had asked her father. "The night is bitter."

Seraphina had peeked around him to see a woman, large with child, sitting on a donkey.

"We've no more room," her father answered.

"Anywhere!" the man begged.

"The stable," her father said, pointing out the cave. "And I wish it were more."

In the starlight now, hours later, Seraphina sees the breath of the donkey. It puffs from the animal like incense rising from the Temple in Jerusalem. A baby's cry pierces the silent night.

"The child is here," Seraphina whispers as she closes the door. A snore is the only response. If Seraphina is cold, the family in the stable must be freezing.

From the dying embers in the fireplace, she lights an oil lamp. Pulling her mantle around her shoulders, she slips out of the house, into the frosty night, and crosses the road, her hands shaking with cold.

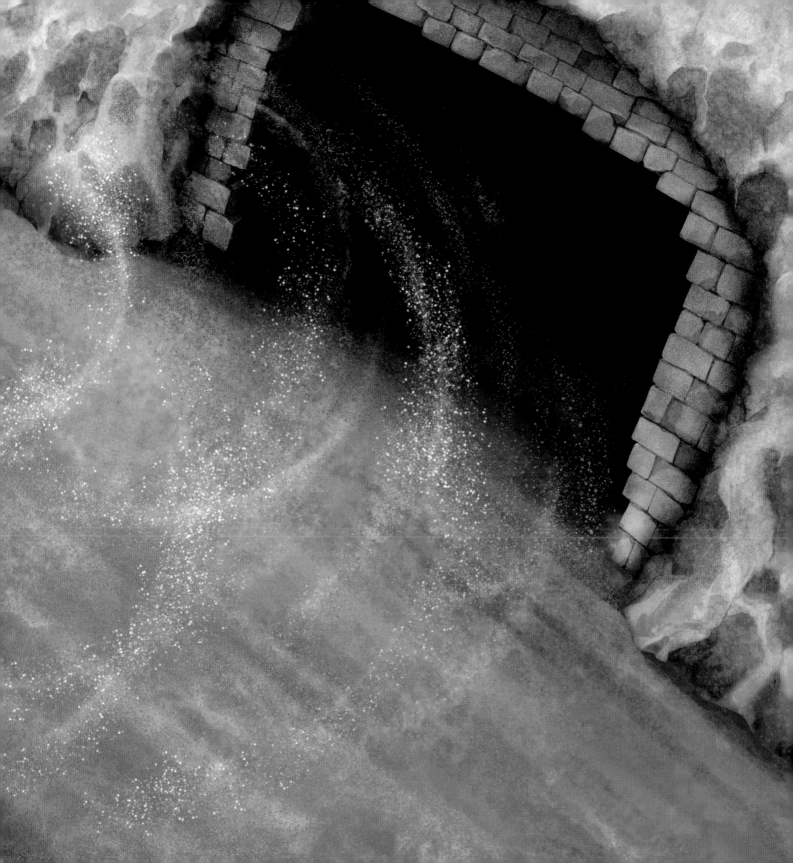

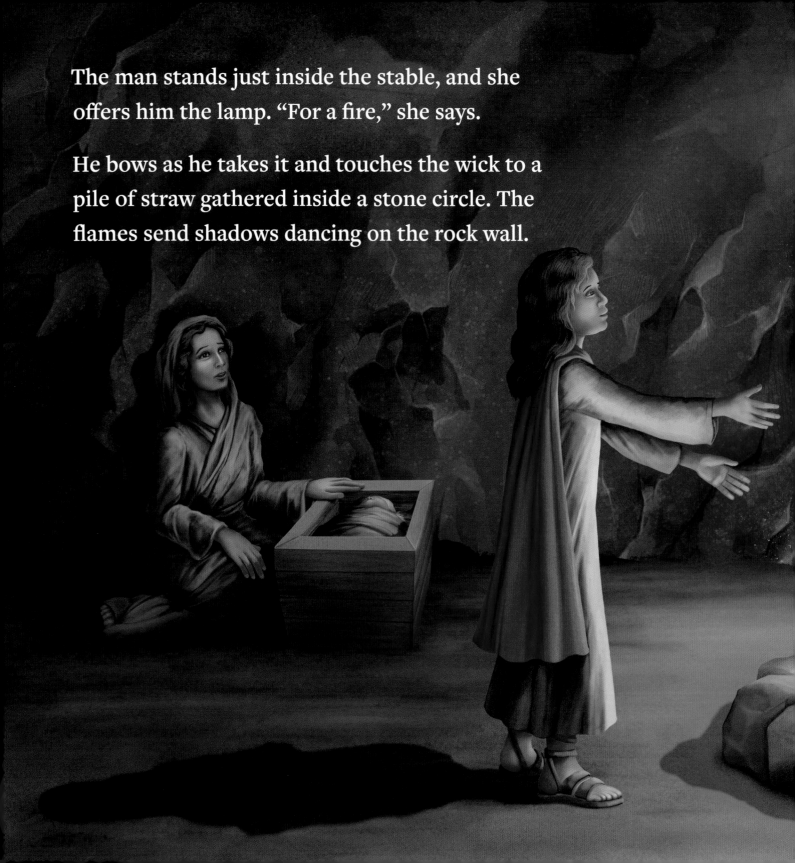

The man stands just inside the stable, and she offers him the lamp. "For a fire," she says.

He bows as he takes it and touches the wick to a pile of straw gathered inside a stone circle. The flames send shadows dancing on the rock wall.

The glow of the fire lights up the face of the mother kneeling next to the manger. She opens her arms wide, inviting Seraphina to come closer.

Seraphina stoops to where the
Baby lies. She slips off her mantle
and tucks it around Him, her touch
as gentle as a bedtime prayer.

The Child smiles in His sleep, flails His arms, and grips her finger with His tiny hand. So warm against her chilled skin!

The heat of His touch rushes up her arm and settles in her chest. The Baby's mother nods, as if she knows a secret.

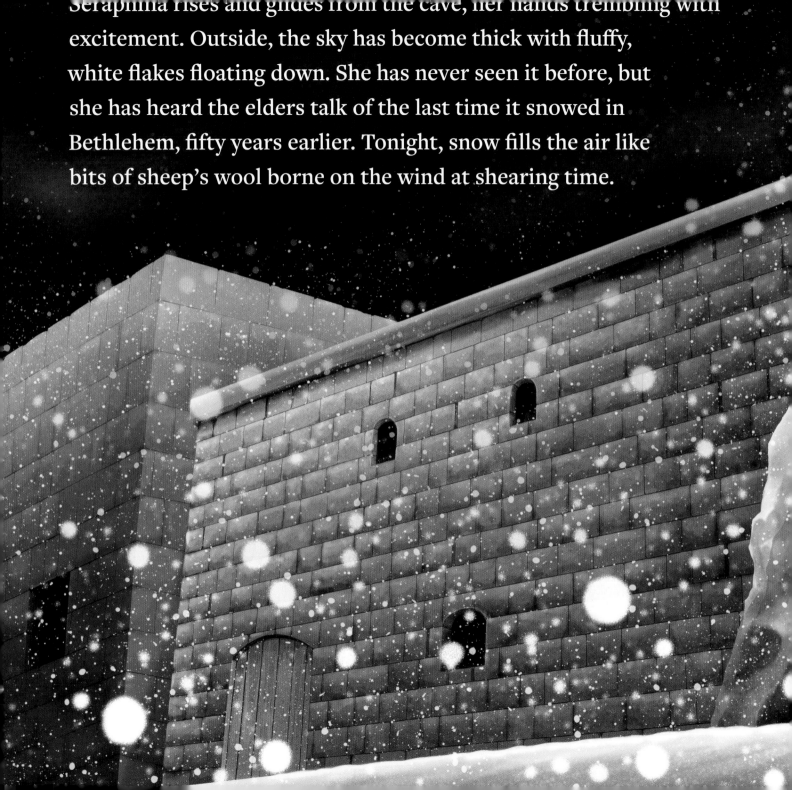

Seraphina rises and glides from the cave, her hands trembling with excitement. Outside, the sky has become thick with fluffy, white flakes floating down. She has never seen it before, but she has heard the elders talk of the last time it snowed in Bethlehem, fifty years earlier. Tonight, snow fills the air like bits of sheep's wool borne on the wind at shearing time.

Still glowing from the touch of the Babe, Seraphina steals back into the house and sails up the ladder.

Under the blanket, she pulls
her shivering little sister close,
heating her, heart to heart.

The snow piles up on the thatched
roof. As Seraphina's eyes slip shut
on this special night, a smile lifts
the corners of her mouth.

The wind seems to hum a heavenly
lullaby as sweet as an angel's song.
Seraphina falls asleep on a pillow of
peace with a fire blazing in her soul,
on this, the warmest night of her life.

The End

The Birth of Christ
— LUKE 2 (ESV) —

In those days a decree went out from Caesar Augustus that all the world should be registered. This was the first registration when Quirinius was governor of Syria. And all went to be registered, each to his own town. And Joseph also went up from Galilee, from the town of Nazareth, to Judea, to the city of David, which is called Bethlehem, because he was of the house and lineage of David, to be registered with Mary, his betrothed, who was with child. And while they were there, the time came for her to give birth. And she gave birth to her firstborn son and wrapped him in swaddling cloths and laid him in a manger, because there was no place for them in the inn.

And in the same region there were shepherds out in the field, keeping watch over their flock by night. And an angel of the Lord appeared to them, and the glory of the Lord shone around them, and they were filled with great fear. And the angel said to them, "Fear not, for behold, I bring you good news of great joy that will be for all the people. For unto you is born this day in the city of David a Savior, who is Christ the Lord. And this will be a sign for you: you will find a baby wrapped in swaddling cloths and lying in a manger." And suddenly there was with the angel a multitude of the heavenly host praising God and saying,

> "Glory to God in the highest,
> and on earth peace among those
> with whom he is pleased!"

When the angels went away from them into heaven, the shepherds said to one another, "Let us go over to Bethlehem and see this thing that has happened, which the Lord has made known to us." And they went with haste and found Mary and Joseph, and the baby lying in a manger. And when they saw it, they made known the saying that had been told them concerning this child. And all who heard it wondered at what the shepherds told them. But Mary treasured up all these things, pondering them in her heart. And the shepherds returned, glorifying and praising God for all they had heard and seen, as it had been told them.

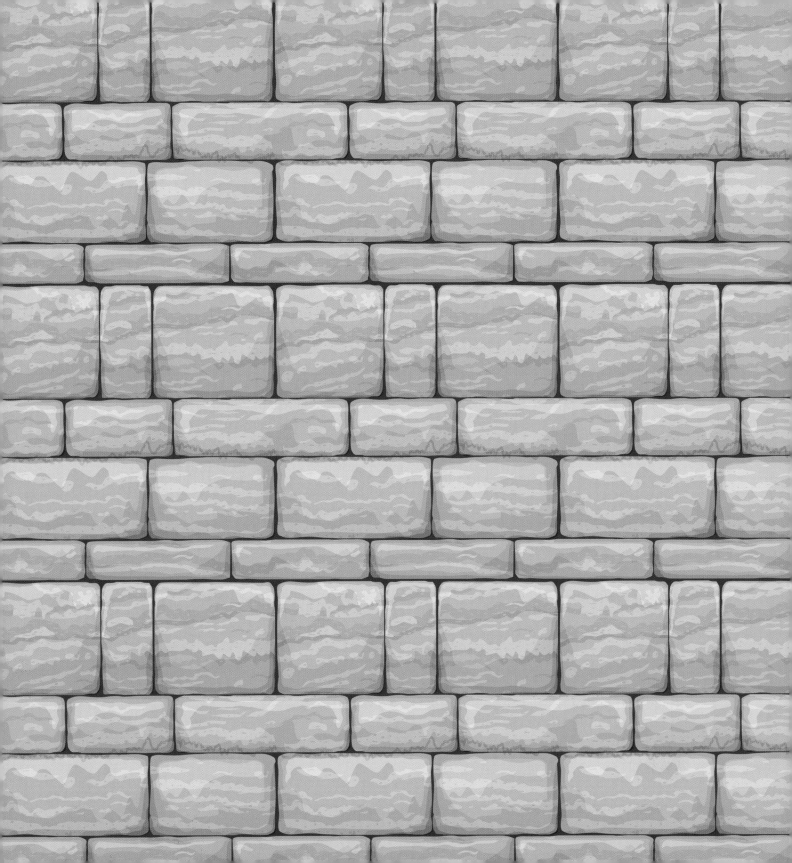